W9-CSS-177

EACH PEACH PEAR PLUM

Janet and Allan Ahlberg

PICTURE PUFFIN

'This is a lovely small book,
well-conceived and very
well-drawn, gentle,
humorous, unsentimental'
    New York Times Book Review

EACH PEACH PEAR PLUM

In this book
With your little eye
Take a look
And play 'I spy'

EACH PEACH PEAR PLUM

Janet and Allan Ahlberg

PUFFIN BOOKS

Each Peach Pear Plum
I spy Tom Thumb

Tom Thumb in the cupboard
I spy Mother Hubbard

Mother Hubbard down the cellar
I spy Cinderella

Cinderella on the stairs
I spy the Three Bears

Three Bears out hunting
I spy Baby Bunting

Baby Bunting fast asleep
I spy Bo-Peep

Bo-Peep up the hill
I spy Jack and Jill

Jack and Jill in the ditch
I spy the Wicked Witch

Wicked Witch over the wood
I spy Robin Hood

Robin Hood in his den
I spy the Bears again

Three Bears still hunting
THEY spy Baby Bunting

Baby Bunting safe and dry
I spy Plum Pie

Plum Pie in the sun
I spy . . .

. . . EVERYONE!

Other Picture Books from Puffin for the Very Young

THE BABY'S BEDTIME BOOK *Kay Chorao*

THE BABY'S BOOK OF BABIES *Kathy Henderson*

THE CHECKUP *Helen Oxenbury*

DEEP IN THE FOREST *Brinton Turkle*

FROGGY GETS DRESSED *London/Remkiewicz*

HUNKY DORY ATE IT *Evans/Stoeke*

MADELINE *Ludwig Bemelmans*

ONE BEAR IN THE PICTURE *Caroline Bucknall*

PADDINGTON'S 123 *Bond/Lobban*

PEEK-A-BOO! *Janet and Allan Ahlberg*

A POCKET FOR CORDUROY *Don Freeman*

THE SNOWY DAY *Ezra Jack Keats*

TRAINS *Anne Rockwell*

WEIRD PARENTS *Audrey Wood*

THE LITTLE DOG LAUGHED AND OTHER NURSERY RHYMES *Lucy Cousins*

PUFFIN BOOKS

Published by the Penguin Group
Penguin Books Ltd, 27 Wrights Lane, London W8 5TZ, England
Penguin Books USA Inc., 375 Hudson Street, New York, New York 10014, USA
Penguin Books Australia Ltd, Ringwood, Victoria, Australia
Penguin Books Canada Ltd, 10 Alcorn Avenue, Toronto, Ontario, Canada M4V 3B2
Penguin Books (NZ) Ltd, 182–190 Wairau Road, Auckland 10, New Zealand

Penguin Books Ltd, Registered Offices: Harmondsworth, Middlesex, England

First published in Great Britain 1978
First published in the USA 1979
Published in Picture Puffins 1986
17 19 20 18

Copyright © Janet and Allan Ahlberg, 1978

Library of Congress catalog card number: 86 – 42569
(CIP data available)

ISBN 0-14-050639-X

Made and printed in Italy by printers srl – Trento

In this book
With your little eye
Take a look
And play 'I spy'

And as the story unfolds,
very young children can spy
familiar nursery characters hiding
in the delightful pictures. There's Tom Thumb,
Jack and Jill, and the Three Bears, as well
as Baby Bunting and a host of others.
A wonderfully entertaining romp.

An American Library Association
Notable Book

ISBN 0-14-050639-X

9 780140 506396

91901

£4.99